Dreams

Dreams
by
Jason Scott

Other works by Jason Scott:
Shift of the Dead (2008)
Hotel Hell (2011)
Shift of the Dead II: Overtime (2011)

Copyright © 2012 by Jason Scott

All rights reserved, including the right to reproduce this book or portions thereof in any form

Characters and places in this work are fictional, or used in a fictional sense. In no way do they represent how any business or individual, living, dead or undead, would or did act in any real life situation.

Chapter 1

She giggled as she pulled him along, sprinting between the houses of a quiet neighborhood street. Her shoulder length hair was dirty blond in the sunlight, but tonight, under the moon, it had the glow of a silvery gold. Johnny squeezed her hand tightly as he ran along side her. The extra weight he'd put on over the years seemed to melt away as he increased his speed. He glanced over at her and gave her a crooked smile. They reached an old, gnarled tree in the far corner of someone's yard. She stopped for just a second to plant a quick kiss on his cheek, not minding the scruff from a few days of not shaving.

"Come on!" she whispered excitedly as her hands found the short boards nailed to tree that formed a crude ladder. She began to climb stealthily up the tree, her small frame barely visible in the moonlight. Johnny began his climb after her, admiring her small tight rear enhanced by the tight, faded blue jeans. He playfully reached a hand to gently push up on her bottom, taking a second to give it a squeeze. He was rewarded with another girlish giggle from above.

Her feet vanished above him as she pulled herself into the crude treehouse. Even in the dim light, Johnny could make out the large pirate flag painted under the window. He pulled himself in after her, the smell of wet wood overwhelming him briefly. A small pair of hands covered his eyes from behind.

"Guess who?" she whispered in his ear, her breath warm and inviting. He took her hand and spun her around, catching her in his arms. As he stared into her sapphire eyes, he felt a warm glow spread throughout his body. For the first time in many years he felt alive. As he tilted his head to go in for the kiss, Johnny watched her pink, thin lips begin to part revealing slightly crooked front teeth that were quickly covered as her mouth closed over his, her tongue darting into his mouth.

"Don't you need to go soon?" she breathed, as their mouths separated. "You can't be late." Still, the blonde girl kissed him again, sending warmth and happiness into his soul. Holding her tightly, Johnny couldn't imagine anything more important than being right here, right now. His hands caressed her back, occasionally finding their way around her side, under the hem of her sweater. Her pale skin was unbelievably soft and she was much warmer than he was.

The sound of a siren cut through the night. The two lovers broke their embrace and peered out into the darkness. Headlights topped by the instantly recognizable red and blue lights of a police car began to grow in the distance. As the lights came closer and siren louder, the couple instinctively crouched down on the rough floor of the treehouse. When the squad car turned the corner near them, the headlights blinded Johnny for a moment. He blinked his eyes rapidly and then started quickly as he looked around and realized he was standing at base of the tree. Spinning around, he looked for her. Seeing that he was alone, he turned his face skyward and went to shout for her.

"Hey...," he began and then stopped, confused. *What in God's name was that beautiful girl's name?* he asked himself. *What in the hell is going on?*

"Goodbye Johnny," came her voice, far away in the darkness. "Don't forget about me! You can't be late, my dear, it's time to go."

Johnny turned as screeching tires got his attention. The squad car was back, this time heading right for him! The headlights made him squint as he tried to find a place to run. The car was only a few feet from him now, and he threw his arms up in a futile attempt to stop the tons of steel from crushing him. The siren blared to life again, so loud it was unbearable. Just as the bumper reached his arms, Johnny cried out.

He sat straight up in his bed, his alarm clock nagging him to get up. He fumbled with the slide lever, succeeding in silencing the alarm. His shade was up, the sunlight bright in his eyes, welcoming him to a new day. With a sigh, Johnny Evans hauled himself from the bed and staggered toward the bathroom. Shrugging off the sweatpants he had slept in, he paused to examine himself in the mirror. His short brown hair stuck out at odd angles around his head. He needed a haircut sooner than later. His piercing gray blue eyes looked tired. Dark circles under them made him look older than his 27 years. Stubble indicated his lack of desire to shave daily. He shook his head in disbelief. *Where does the time go? Feel like just yesterday that I turned 18.*

He quickly showered. The hot water relaxed him and almost drove the remnants of his dream from his memory. However, as he washed his hair, the flowery scent of the shampoo brought the image of the blonde girl rushing back into his mind. He sighed. *How come I can only find love in my dreams?*

He finished his shower and dressed quickly. Grabbing a plum as he walked out the door, Johnny sped through the hallway of his apartment building, pausing only to check the ancient metal mailbox near the outer door. Stepping into the sunlight, he squinted his eyes against the invading brightness. His black Charger stood out amongst the sea of beat up sedans and mini vans that overflowed the parking lot. He breathed a sigh of relief that his baby remained unscratched. He'd parked in the corner of the lot, as usual. That way he only had to worry about one person parking next to him and carelessly throwing their car door into his beauty. Of course, being next to the grass meant the Charger also had to contend with the army of children walking by it as they scurried out of the dozen buildings that made up the apartment complex.

Following his daily ritual, he said a quick "Thank you" to God as he sat down in his dream ride. It was one of the few luxuries that Johnny allowed himself. The V-8 roared to life with a throaty rumble that warmed his soul. Depressing the clutch, he backed out of his parking spot. Creeping onto the street, he quickly worked through the gears and sped up the ramp onto the highway. Settling in at 70mph, Johnny, rolled down the window and enjoyed his ride to work. It would be the only part of the work day that he could enjoy. All too soon, he pulled into the parking ramp of Walker Industries and found himself a corner spot.

With a sigh, Johnny plodded into the building and joined the small crowd in the elevator heading to the third floor.

"What's up, buddy?" asked Dean Drake, one of Johnny's friends and coworkers.

"Just another day in paradise," answered Johnny as he did every morning. "We doing anything tonight?"

"Party at Colt's going on. You want me to pick you up?"

"What time?"

"I dunno. 9ish?"

"Sounds good."

Dean was always willing to drive if Johnny was willing to go out. He was the same age as Johnny but much more outgoing. Puerto Rican, his dark skin and darker eyes always made him popular with the ladies. His easy smile made him fun to be around, and Johnny enjoyed his company. They'd become friends shortly after Dean started at Walker Industries and since sharing a drunken night on the town a few months ago, the two men were inseparable most weekends.

The elevator dinged to announced their arrival on floor number three. The two friends made their way to adjacent cubicles on the far side of the room. The room was filled with the excitement of Friday and the smell of coffee. There were thirty or so cubes on this floor, plus the offices of the big wigs. Glancing around the room, Johnny caught the eye of Colton Standish and waved a good morning. Colt smiled and made his way toward Johnny, an extra cup of coffee in hand.

Colton was a tall man, with piercing blue eyes and spiked dirty blonde hair. He was dressed in an upscale polo shirt without a single wrinkle in his attire. Perfectly straight and gleaming white teeth flashed at Johnny as

Colton set the coffee carefully on Johnny's desk.

"You coming over tonight? There are going to be some fine ladies to chat up," said Colton, grinning.

"Yeah, Dean and I are going to make it."

"Dean, huh?" frowned Colton. "You need to keep him in line then." Dean tended to party hard, while Colton was always in total control. Johnny enjoyed his friendship with both men, but hated having to be the man in the middle all the time.

"Of course," sighed Johnny, "I'll make sure that Dean doesn't do anything to embarrass you."

"Thanks! Hey, you want to come bowling with me Saturday night?"

"Don't you bowl in a league?" asked Johnny.

"That's on Wednesdays. Saturday we are just going for fun. Miranda will bring a friend. It'll be fun." Miranda was Colton's girlfriend. The two of them were always trying to set him up, but their choices tended to be a little too snooty for Johnny.

"Maybe. Let's see how I feel after tonight," laughed Johnny, successfully putting off that decision.

Glancing at his diamond and gold wristwatch, Colton began to head toward his own cubicle. "Better get to work before Felix starts cracking the whip."

Right on cue, Felix Anderson, the supervisor, shouted to the room, "Come on, people. Let's get to work. Those robots aren't going to program themselves. We've got numbers to hit." The short man was in his early 40's, sported a gray buzzcut and a smile. He was a relentless cheerleader. "We're going to have a great day!"

Shaking his head, Johnny sat down and began working on the new sequence for the J-38. The J-38 was one of many robotic assemblers that Walker Industries produced. It was slightly larger than a man and consisted of multiple arms and actuator that allowed it to perform various human like movements. While the guys on the 4th floor got to do the magic and create the language that the J-38 spoke, Johnny and the other drones here on the 3rd floor worked to adjust the minute details that would let the J-38 efficiently build whatever the current contract called for. Right now he was working on a command sequence that had the J-38 taking a bolt from a hopper and then rotating it's wrist to precisely screw it into the hole while a second arm placed and held the nut in place. Truthfully, Johnny didn't even know what the machine was building. He didn't care either. The work was mind numbingly dull. Often he was correcting measurements in the hundredths of millimeters. Once he had the computer simulation running at 99% efficiency, then he would get to go down to the ground floor and test it out with the real machines. Well, he'd get to watch as someone else tested his work and then either approved it or sent it back to him for more corrections. Either way, when he was finished, he'd be assigned another similar piece of code to write.

The day dragged on. At the mid-morning break, Johnny chatted with his friend, Jose Fernandez about politics, while Dean joined a large chunk of the office staff that headed outside to have a cigarette.

"You can't keep coddling the Super Rich!" argued Jose, "They need to contribute their fair share!"

"Their fair share? Almost half the people in this country don't pay ANY taxes!" shot back Johnny, "You think that the guy that busted his ass to get an education and great job should give another ten percent of his $200,000 salary to the government so that they can redistribute it to a pair of welfare mothers that have a half dozen kids from a half dozen fathers?"

"That's harsh, man," replied Jose, "I understand what you're sayin', but it's harsh."

"Harsh or not, it's true. We should be having people on welfare either get ten hours of job training or schooling or community service each week to keep collecting. Anything to give us a chance to stop the cycle!" answered Johnny.

"You can't blame every poor person for their situation. That person making $200,00 a year probably had rich parents who paid for their college education," countered Jose.

"Your parents didn't pay for your schooling and you have a decent job!"

"That's true, but I'm a rare case. I know plenty of smart Chicanos that never escaped the neighborhood."

"Still, we need to make sure that welfare isn't a profitably way of life."

Jose shushed him and pointed toward one of the women walking toward them. "Quiet, man, if Shelly hears you, she'll report you for harassment or discrimination or whatever."

"Screw Shelly!" fired back Johnny.

"No, really, she will. A year ago, Evan Wakos was saying how he was pissed that his sister in law got a $13,000 tax return and Shelly went to the bosses and he got canned for bad mouthing welfare folks."

"What a great country we have! You can't debate things without fear of losing your job," spat Johnny. "Screw it!" With that, Johnny downed the remainder of his coffee, refilled his cup and stomped back to his cubicle.

The rest of the day went by at the speed of a glacier. Johnny let his mind wander as he worked. His thoughts kept coming to rest on the girl from his dreams. *Why can't I find someone like her in real life?* he sighed. Finally the end of his shift came and Johnny dodged everyone, nodded a quick "See you later!" to Dean and practically ran out of the building. He jumped into his Charger and sped toward his apartment. He spent the next few hours checking his Facebook, reading science fiction on his kindle, and watching reality television via Netflix. Johnny was bored to death with his life.

Chapter 2

Johnny stood outside his apartment building, waiting patiently for his ride to arrive. His Beauty sat parked in the corner of the lot, silent. She wouldn't be going anywhere tonight. One of Johnny's hard and fast rules is that you didn't drink and drive. He knew it was foolish to object to committing the act himself, but still ride with someone who had been drinking, but he followed his rule nonetheless.

Dressed in khakis and a tan dress shirt, Johnny was ready for Colt's party. He didn't really want to go, but at the same time, he didn't really have a reason to not go. He debated with himself for a few minutes and actually decided to just turn in for the night. He was in the process of texting his decline, when Dean pulled up in his SUV. Hesitating only a second, Johnny canceled his text and hopped into Dean's vehicle.

"You ready to party, brother?" asked Dean. "We should have a bunch of fine honeys to choose from."

"I'm ready, my friend," said Johnny, stepping up into the SUV. "Let's roll."

Dean sped through the night, his earring glinting in the lights from the oncoming traffic. He was dressed in black pants and a white shirt with top few buttons undone. A gold chain and fancy watch completed his look. Running his hand through his short black hair, Dean chatted about football and his fantasy team. Johnny listened politely, with no real commitment to the conversation. Ten minutes later they parked on the street in front of the Standish residence, a moderate ranch style home in a late Colonial style.

Johnny scanned the room as soon as they entered. He spotted a few familiar faces and nodded a hello to each. While Dean immediately made himself a Captain and Coke, Johnny found himself a bottle of an amber beer. Within minutes, Dean was chatting up a curly haired blonde. Johnny left the two of them to a semblance of privacy and wandered over to the host.

"Thanks for having me tonight, Colt," said Johnny. "And, of course, you too, Miranda."

"We're so glad you came, Johnny!" exclaimed Miranda, her dark eyes flitting around the room. "Have you met Joanne yet?" she asked, waving a dark haired woman over.

"Miranda, don't," scolded Colt, "Johnny can find his own date."

"Well, he hasn't so far," slurred Miranda, breaking into a fit of giggles.

Johnny tried to keep the frown off his face and failed. Colt noticed and rolled his eyes toward Miranda and then mouthed an apology to him. Joanne was introduced to Johnny and then the two of them were left awkwardly alone. Johnny kept us his end of their conversation, but two minutes into it, he knew he had no interest in this woman. She was nice enough and fairly pretty, but she had no intellectual spark. When she excused herself to go to the restroom, he used the opportunity to escape outside.

Several people were sitting on the front steps smoking cigarettes. Avoiding the cloud of foul smelling smoke, Johnny made his way to the curb and leaned up against Dean's SUV. The night air was cool and the moon was shining brightly. He tilted the bottle back and drained the remainder of the beer. He carefully set the empty bottle down on the curb.

"Shouldn't litter, brother," said a gravelly voice from behind him. Johnny spun around, he foot catching the bottle and sending it bouncing into the street, miraculously staying intact.

A man in his early forties, dressed mostly in black stared back at him. A mop of curly dirty blonde hair and a dark goatee gave the man a menacing look.

"I was going to take it with me," explained Johnny, stammering slightly. He stepped into the street to retrieve the bottle. When he turned back around, the man was gone. Confused, Johnny looked around, even circled the SUV, but no sign of the mysterious stranger was to be found. A shiver passed down his spine. He took the empty bottle with him and went back into the house.

The rest of the night went as he expected. Joanne was miffed that he had left without telling her, and ignored him the rest of the night, to his delight. He sat on a stool near the kitchen counter and made idle chat as the party goers came to refill their drinks. Colt finished off the night as he always did. He raised his right arm in a mock Nazi salute and then performed a front kick, demonstrating that he could still bring his foot high enough to make contact with his extended fingers. Johnny smiled. In his mind, he always imaged that all those years of bowling had stretched Colt's right arm making it easier for him to perform this trick.

Dean was bringing the blonde home with him. Johnny accepted the back seat of the SUV and stayed silent on the ride home. Dean dropped him off, bumped knuckles with him through the window and then sped off with the blonde laughing. Johnny took a minute to check on his Charger before going upstairs and heading to bed.

Chapter 3

They were in a diner. It was dark outside. The beautiful blonde girl sat across from him, picking at her food with her fork. Fried eggs, breakfast potatoes and a half eaten sausage mirrored his own plate. She stabbed the piece of sausage and took a bite, leaving the rest on her fork.

"So, what are we going to do next?" she asked him, "I've got all night."

"Whatever you want, Jane," he answered. *Jane! That's her name! How do I know that?* thought Johnny.

"We could go back to your place?" she said coyly, as he felt her foot creeping up his leg.

Confused and stalling for time, Johnny took a huge bite of his potatoes, then cringing he bit into a large bit of pepper that had been hidden. She laughed with him as he quickly downed half a glass of water.

"Do I scare you that much, Johnny?" she asked, letting a grin creep across her face. Her pale blue eyes stared into him. She flipped her blonde hair and leaned back in the booth, placing her bare feet on the table. "We can always just stay here." She crossed her arms over her chest. She was dressed in a white tank top and faded jean shorts. He noticed a small round scar on her knee.

He started to answer her, when suddenly, sunlight poured into the diner through the window behind her head. Her hair lit up like a golden mane. He looked down at his plate. A half eaten taco and some refried beans surprised him. He looked back to Jane, and realized they were now sitting in a small Mexican restaurant.

"Aren't dreams wonderful? We can do whatever we want," she said. She crawled over the table and sat facing him. He wrapped her arms around his neck and leaned forward, tilted her head, and kissed her. He lost himself in the kiss for a moment, until a scream jolted him back to reality. A dirty middle aged man had drawn a gun and was coming towards them.

"Don't anyone make any stupid moves!" he ordered with a slight German accent. Pointing the gun at red haired woman behind the bar, he demanded the money from the cash register. Another patron quickly stood and elbowed the robber in the small of the back. The robber swung the gun around and a shot rang out.

    Jane cried out, her body thrown off of Johnny. A blood stain quickly grew across her white shirt. Johnny screamed and reached for her. From the corner of his eye, he caught a glimpse of a man in a black leather vest subdue the would-be robber. Jane's eyes grew glassy and her breathing turned into a raspy panting. He held her and cried as the life left her body. A wail forced itself from his soul.

    Then he woke up.

Chapter 4

"That's some messed up shit," said Dean. "Most guys don't dream of kissing a girl and then her dying in his arms. How much did you drink last night?"

"Just a few beers. Really. I went to bed right after you dropped me off," answered Johnny.

"Sounds a little loco to me, Chico," said Jose, laughing. "You need to give up the beer and drink tequila with me. There won't be enough of your mind left to give you crazy dreams."

"It was so real," said Johnny, shaking his head, "I wake up every morning missing her."

"I woke up this morning trying to figure out how to get that blonde out of my house," laughed Dean, "Had a good time, though."

"Come on, guys, breaks over!" Felix Anderson said enthusiastically, while clapping his hands together, "Let's go, let's go."

"Doesn't that guy ever slow down?" whispered Dean to Johnny. "Someone should spike his coffee."

"Shh," replied Johnny, "Someone will get ideas."

"Someone should."

The men went back to their respective cubicles and got back to work. Johnny's thoughts continued to go back to his strange dreams. Half rising from his chair, he spotted the supervisor, Felix, chatting excitedly about football on the other side of the room. Johnny opened a new window and searched the internet for "Weird Dreams."

After investigating several links, he found an interesting article by a man named Adam Graves. Graves claimed to be a Paranormal Investigator. His biography was impressive and included a link to a book he'd written, "Hotel Hell." The "Dreams" article hypothesized that when we dream, our minds crossed over into another reality. Mr. Graves stated that several of those plagued by ghosts had reported strange dreams that turned out to be connected with their haunting. *Am I being haunted by Jane? She doesn't seem dangerous?* pondered Johnny. Then he snorted at himself in disgust. *Why am I thinking of the girl from my dreams as a real person. I must be losing it.* Still, he was intrigued enough to want to know more about Adam Graves. He clicked on the link and purchased an ebook version of "Hotel Hell."

"Evans!" boomed Felix, causing Johnny to jump in his chair, "How is shopping online getting your work done?"

Johnny bit back the response about how was Felix's talking about football all day wasn't helping anyone either. Instead, he stayed silent and nodded.

"Can we please get back to work? You are being paid to work one hundred percent of your shift, not eighty percent. Would you take eighty percent of your pay?" continued Felix. When Johnny did not argue, but nodded in agreement, Felix moved on.

Johnny felt his phone buzz in his pocket. Risking the wrath of Felix, he pulled it out and glanced at it.

Dean: Nice one, dork!

Dean's quiet chuckle drifted over from his cubicle. With a sigh, Johnny got back to work.

Arriving home that night, Johnny settled into the corner of his couch with his Kindle. "Hotel Hell by Adam Graves" was at the top of the Most Recent list. It told the story of some teenagers that had went to an abandoned hotel to have a party. A ghostly girl that had died at the hotel years before plagued their visit. Johnny became enthralled with the story. Several hours later, he looked at the clock and realized it was almost 11:00pm. He'd finished the book in one sitting. Before turning in for the night, he fired off an email to Adam Graves.

Mr. Graves,

My name is Johnny Evans. I just finished reading Hotel Hell. I enjoyed it very much. How much of that book was fiction and how much was based on real events? I've read your bio and your Paranormal Investigators business seems to get legit reviews.

I've been having some odd dreams lately that might be of interest to you. I am having reoccurring dreams of a girl that I do not know. In each dream, it ends with something violent occurring. I'm almost afraid to go to sleep at night, yet I cannot wait to see her again! It probably seems crazy to you, but after reading your article on dreams, I felt compelled to write to you. If you are interested in hearing more, I would appreciate speaking to you.

Sincerely,
John Evans

Johnny hesitated a minute, feeling foolish. With a shrug of his shoulders, he hit "Send." Crawling into bed, he wondered what he would dream of tonight.

Chapter 5

"Johnny!"

Jane's voice was like a song to him. It was like a song that you had heard your entire life and knew what it was the second you heard the first note. Johnny blinked his eyes and looked around. He was at an amusement park. He felt the sun beat down on him, the humidity oppressive. He was dressed in jean shorts and a tan t-shirt. Sunglasses covered his eyes and kept the glaring sunlight to a minimum. They were walking toward a long row of booths containing games and rides. Jane walked beside him, holding his right hand. Her tiny palm lost in his, feeling slightly clammy.

She was gorgeous. Shoulder length reddish hair not quite fitting her skin tone. Brilliant blue eyes smiled at him. She wore a low cut tropical blue top and black shorts. He noticed her brightly painted toenails and her strap style sandals.

"Let's go on the boat ride!" she said excitedly, reminding him of a child.

"Sure," he answered, his voice sounding strange to his ears.

They stopped at the first booth and entered the queue line. One by one an empty brown boat would appear from behind the dangling curtains, round the corner near the front of the booth, and then stop as the riders at the top of a small staircase carefully stepped inside. Once the dark haired woman working the ride was satisfied the riders were situated, she would motion to a man dressed all in blue so he could press a button at the control panel and send the boat into the dark tunnel.

As they transverse the line, Johnny removed his sunglasses and slid the bow into the collar of his shirt, letting the glasses hang down on his chest. Jane, he noticed, had hers perched atop of her head. She snuggled close to him and he released her hand and put his arm around her shoulder, pulling her tight. She looked up at him and smiled, her teeth perfect and her smile wide. Soon they were perched at the top of the staircase waiting for their boat.

"How you guys doing?" asked the ride operator, her eyes weary.

"We're great!" exclaimed Jane, "Is the ride scary?" she asked cautiously.

"Not too bad, honey. I'm sure this man of yours will protect you," laughed the woman. "Now, in you go." She ushered the two of them into the waiting boat.

Johnny stepped in first, and holding her hand, helped Jane in next to him. The ride operator put out her arm and stopped the family in line behind them from entering the boat. "Let's leave these two lovebirds ride alone." Johnny nodded a thank you to her. Jane wriggled closer to him as the boat entered the dark tunnel.

The boat glided through the water in total darkness. An uneasy feeling grew in Johnny's throat. He grasped Jane by the hand and squeezed tightly. He wasn't going to let her go. Ever. After what seemed like an eternity, the boat emerged from the dark corridor and into a dimly lit tunnel that seemed to go on forever. It was lined with lanterns that gave off a strange green light. The walls were dark stone, carved with griffins, gargoyles and other magical creatures. Peering into the darkness, Johnny was relieved to make out the faint outline of another boat ahead of them. Jane shivered and tucked herself into him.

The blank stares of the stone creatures were accompanied by low moans and other inhuman growls. A cold wind tickled the back of his neck, a shiver traveled down his spine. Excited screams pierced the blanket of silence as the boat in front of them dipped out of sight. The sound of rushing water began to fill the cavern. As they cleared the last of the green lanterns, the boat began to buffet back and forth. The light faded to nothing. Johnny and Jane moved as close as possible in the tiny boat and clung to each other. Johnny felt his stomach drop away as the boat lunged forward down a steep incline in total darkness. It splashed at the bottom of the hill, spraying them both with icy water. Jane's musical laughter echoed throughout the ride.

The boat floated into a room that was a tomb, like the inside of a pyramid. Stained yellow stones lined the walls, covered in Egyptian hieroglyphics. Anubis was chasing after a terrified slave. Screams echoed throughout the tomb. Flickering torchlight cast eerie shadows. Johnny frowned as the walls began to melt away.

"No, Johnny! Stay with me!" pleaded Jane.

Forcing himself to concentrate he squeezed his eyes shut. He felt her hand hold him tighter. He opened his eyes and found himself staring at the ceiling of his bedroom. He quickly closed them again and willed himself back into the dream. Now he could hear carnival music and feel Jane pressed tightly against him. He very slowly opened his eyes. Her smile brightened and she kissed him fiercely.

Before he could ask what had happened, shouts and screams filled the air. Johnny looked up and saw the Meteor ride collapsing and falling toward them. He tried to pull Jane out of the way, but wasn't fast enough. Thick steel girders covered her and several others. Her hand was pulled from his grasp. He frantically began moving the rubble call her name over and over.

"Stay back!" shouted the blonde man, dressed all in black.

Johnny woke up sobbing.

Chapter 6

"I'm telling you, it was as real as being here right now," explained Johnny for the dozenth time.

"I think you drank too much, bro," answered Jose, "You had one too many last night and had a vivid nightmare."

"Why do I keep dreaming of the same girl over and over then? And why does she always die?"

"Johnny," Jose said, lowering his voice, "it's pretty obvious. You're feeling alone. You're looking for love and you just can't find it. Your subconscious is just screwing with you. Whether it's seeing Colt happy with his wife or watching Dean screw everything that moves, you're feeling left out or left behind."

Johnny snorted, "Really? That's your explanation?"

"Yes, it is. Think about it. You are so desperate for love that your mind has created your perfect girlfriend. She's pretty, loves you without reason, and then mysteriously vanishes before the illusion can shatter."

"I guess," said Johnny slowly, "I guess that could make sense. But what about the man in black?"

"He represents reality. As you lose her in each dream, reality is rearing its ugly head."

"But I saw him in real life! Outside the office and outside Colt's party."

"Of course you did. Your mind borrowed his likeness and used it in your dreams. Wouldn't surprise me at all if you saw your dream girl sometime in the past either, even if you don't remember it," analyzed Jose. "It's all explainable."

"But..." stammered Johnny.

"But nothing. Take it for what it is and move on. By analyzing it, chances are the dreams will cease now."

As Jose walked away, Johnny was distraught with the thought of Jane not visiting his dreams anymore. *I was so sure there was something to this. So sure that the dreams were supernatural.*

"Evans! Quit the daydreaming!" boomed Felix Anderson, not bothering to stop, "Let's get back to work, buddy."

The rest of the work day dragged by. Johnny avoided his friends. He has no desire to rehash his experience again. He was tired and confused. When the clock struck quitting time, he dashed to his car before anyone could talk to him.

On the way home he stopped at the neighborhood liquor store and selected a six pack of a dark microbrew. He had the first bottle open before he had his front door shut. He had that bottle finished and another started in less than five minutes. An hour later, six empty bottles stood in a neat row on his kitchen table. Johnny lay down on the couch and fell fast asleep. He didn't dream.

Chapter 7

Johnny awoke to his phone ringing. Glancing at the clock, he was surprised to see that it was only nine o'clock. His head still swimming from the beer, he answered the phone.

"Hello?"

"Johnny boy! Big party at my place going on. Get your ass down here!" said Dean, excitedly.

"No, man, I'm staying in."

"No, it's the weekend and you're coming over."

"No, I already had some beer. I can't drive," argued Johnny.

"I'll come get you."

"No, you're drunk already and it's your party. I'll just stay home."

"Like hell you will. Joanna will be there to pick you up in 15 minutes. Wear a tropical shirt. We're having a luau."

"Who is Joanna?" asked Johnny.

"Just be ready," laughed Dean, hanging up before Johnny could argue anymore.

Johnny ran a brush through his hair and found his lone Hawaiian shirt in the closet and put it on. He brushed his teeth and wiped the sleep from his eyes. He was just getting on his shoes when someone began knocking on his door. He open the door to find a beautiful woman standing there. She had wide eyes and an easy smile. Deep cleavage drew his eyes down. She was dressed in a short, orange tropical dress.

"You ready to go?" she questioned, her voice had a hint of New Yorker in it.

"Ready to go. Johnny Evans," he stated, offering his hand. She shook it vigorously.

"Joanna Anderson. Let's roll."

Still feeling woozy from his previous drinks, Johnny bounced slightly off the door frame as he struggled to get his door locked behind him. Expecting to see a disapproving look when he turned back to Joanna, instead she was smiling and holding back a friendly giggle.

"You aren't going to pass out in my car, are you?" she laughed. "Or worse?"

"Nope, I'll be good," slurred Johnny, "Lead the way!"

He locked his eyes on her swaying hips and followed her to the parking lot.

The Luau was in full swing by the time he arrived. A few people were seated around the kitchen table inside, but the majority were scattered around the backyard in small groups. Bright floral prints and leis seemed to be the dress code and fruity drinks of all colors were being consumed. The Beach Boys were playing in the background.

"Johnny!" yelled Dean, "About damn time you got your lazy ass here!" He pressed a beer into Johnny's hand. "I trust the ride was acceptable?"

"Very," smiled Johnny, throwing caution to the wind and draining half the beer in a single swallow. "She was very acceptable," he laughed.

"And very single," added Dean.

"No boyfriend? Nice!"

"And as of last week, no girlfriend either," laughed Dean.

Johnny raised an eyebrow, "So I don't have a chance anyway?"

Dean laughed again, "No, bro, she likes both. Go for it."

Johnny finished off his beer and accepted another before wading into the crowd to find Joanna. He spotted her chatting with two guys camped out on the lawn next to a tiki torch. She waved as he approached and introduced him.

"Johnny, these are my friends Stanley and Robby."

"Nice to meet you," slurred Johnny, shaking first the hand of the smaller man with the wild beard and the bright red streak in his hair and then repeated it with the taller, bulkier man, again with a full beard and a more conventional haircut. The larger man looked slightly uncomfortable.

"Ooh, he's got a strong grip, Robby. You better keep an eye on him," teased Stan.

Joanna laughed as Johnny flushed red with embarrassment. She leaned over and whispered to him, "Don't worry about Stanley. He hits on every cute guy. But he's been with Robby for almost a year now. He's just seeing how you will react." Johnny noticed that Joanna smelled like fresh fruit and took the opportunity to get closer to whisper his appreciation into her ear.

The four of them chatted and enjoyed several drinks. Joanna even convinced him to dance with her. The alcohol was going to his head faster than before. He laughed loudly as Stan ground against Robby dancing next to them. The music stopped for a brief moment.

"Game time in ten minutes!" yelled Dean. The party cheered him. "But first, Jello Shots!"

Joanna quickly grabbed a tray filled with small paper cups containing Jello Shots of every color of the rainbow. Taking one for herself, she seductively used her tongue to consume it. She smiled and passed two shots to Johnny, giving him a quick peck on the cheek as she went by. "Be right back, sweetie."

Johnny smiled and caught Dean's eye and raised his shot to say thanks to his friend. Dean returned the gesture. Johnny sucked down both shots. The fruity flavor masked any alcohol they contained. Stan and Robby were now making out, so he wandered away to get himself another beer. He stopped to chat with Colt and Miranda, before becoming aggravated with the way that Miranda kept hinting to Colt that it was time for them to go. Her dark eyes were beginning to get angry, so Johnny kept moving. He finished another beer, grabbed another, and then spotted Jose. He had just sat down next to him when Dean loudly proclaimed, "Let the games begin!"

Johnny's head was spinning as he sat next to Jose. They chatted about upcoming fantasy movies while Dean explained the rules of the first game.

"We are now going to play the world famous Box Game! I'm going to take this cereal box that has the top flaps cut off. The rules are simple. You have to pick this box up using only your teeth. Both your feet have to stay touching the ground and no other body parts can touch the ground, walls or anything else other than yourself. After everyone has a chance, we cut a few inches off the box and go again until we have a winner! Get it? If not, you will soon," rattled off Dean, as if reciting a favorite story.

"No way I'm doing that," stated Jose.

"Me neither," said Johnny, who looked up to see Joanna holding her hand out to him. Her eyes smiled at him. With a sigh, Johnny got up and unsteadily stood in line behind her. He felt the beer fogging his thoughts. He concentrated on Joanna's straight reddish hair and occasionally let his eyes continue down her short orange dress.

At the front of the line, Colt was the first contestant. He set his feet a good distance apart, placed his hands on his knees, and bent over, easily grabbing the box. The audience cheered loudly as Colt replaced the box. Miranda was next. She seemed embarrassed. She was wearing a tight maroon dress which threatened to ride up and she tried to find a way to get the box without bending over. She managed to squat while using her hands to keep her dress in place. She clenched the box with her teeth and stood quickly. Again, the crowd cheered. She tossed her jet black hair and walked to the back of the line, not smiling.

Joanna was next. She kicked off her sandals and barefooted, let her feet slide far apart. Hands on her ankles, she easily bent over completed the challenge. Johnny couldn't resist the view he had behind her. He stumbled forward for his turn. He started by trying to spread his feet, but his tendons cried out in protest. Trying a new technique, he placed one foot well in front of the other and placed both hands on top of his front foot. He was able to get the box into his teeth, but overburdened with alcohol, he fell trying to get up. Laughing, he picked himself off the ground and placed the box down for the next person. Excusing himself, he went inside to use the bathroom.

After relieving himself, Johnny went back outside to watch the rest of the Box Game. Joanna was up again, this time attempting to pick up a much shorter box. She smiled when she saw Johnny.

"Honey, sit right here and guard my backside," she laughed. She pushed him into a chair and positioned herself in front of him. Hiking up her dress, she bent forward and grabbed the box. Johnny did his best to not stare, feeling heat rising to his cheeks again. As the crowd applauded, she rewarded him with a kiss on the cheek. She giggled and sat down half on his lap. Johnny slipped an arm around her waist and looked her in the eyes. She leaned down to him and they kissed.

After a moment, they broke their embrace and Johnny turned his attention back to the game. A small girl with dirty blonde hair was bent over in front of him attempting to grab the box. Trying to get back up she leaned forward a bit too far and tumbled over, giggling. Sitting on the floor, she tossed the box to Dean. Her eyes widened in surprise as she saw Johnny.

"Jane!" he cried out.

"Johnny?" she said quietly, trembling in fear, "What the hell?" She scrambled to her feet and ran inside the house.

"Who was that?" asked Joanna quietly, "An old girlfriend?"

"Sort of," answered Johnny, shaking.

Joanna stood up, "Well, go talk to her. I'll be here when you get back."

Johnny sat still for a full minute, and then quietly went inside the house.

He slipped inside the house and looked around. The girl was nowhere to be found. Creeping up the stairs, he called out, "Hello?" over and over. He heard the front door open close with a bang. He hurried down the stairs and darted outside. She was scurrying down the driveway.

"Hey! Jane! Wait!" shouted Johnny, running after her.

"Go away!" she yelled, turning to confront him. Her cheeks were flushed with anger and her body shook with fear. "I don't know you. Leave me alone!"

Stunned, Johnny stood statue still as the blonde girl crossed the street and entered the park. *Maybe I am crazy?* he thought. He was still staring at the spot she had vanished into when a voice startled him.

"Aren't you going after her, brother?"

It was the man in black. Dressed in a black vest, tattoos covering his arms, he glared at Johnny with piercing blue eyes. The dirty mop of blond curled hair clung tightly to his deeply tanned face. His lip curled in disgust behind his goatee.

"Who the hell ARE you?" said Johnny, intending to yell, but instead the words came out as a whisper. "Who the hell is she?"

"I'm just here to observe. If you want to find out who she is, I suggest you go ask her." The man gave a slight shrug and leaned back against a car, making no move to chase after the girl himself. When Johnny still did not move, the man waved his hand as if shooing a fly away. "Go on. Go get her while you can."

Johnny sprang into action. He sprinted through the darkness into the park. He found her sitting alone on a swing, staring at the ground. She raised her head and locked her eyes onto his. He approached carefully, deliberately.

"Hey," whispered Johnny.

"Hey," she answered, her voice child like.

"Have we met before?"

"Well..." she trailed off.

"Oh my God. You've had the dreams too!" he stammered out.

"I've seen you in my dreams," she confirmed. "Each time I dream of you, I am so confused. They start off as sweet dreams and end in nightmares. Are you here to kill me?"

"Kill you? No, no no. In my dreams, I'm always trying to save you," he answered. "Is your name really Jane?"

"Yes, it is. Jane Jordan. And you're Johnny?" she asked.

"Yeah, Johnny Evans. This is too weird," he said, plopping down into the swing next to her. That sat in silence for a few moments. Jane slowly reached out her small hand and grasped his tightly. Their eyes met.

"What do we do now?" she asked him.

"I don't know -" started Johnny, but he was interrupted by the sound of gunfire near the park entrance. Both of them jumped up and looked around confused. A large man burst forth from the shadows. The Man in Black.

"Run!" he screamed to Jane as he took hold of Johnny by the arm. Pressing a gun into Johnny's hand, he yelled, "They're coming!"

Jane whimpered and ran into the woods of the park. Johnny tried to follow her but the blond man held his arm in a steely grip. Two men dressed in strange, dark uniforms ran full speed into the park. They didn't seem to be carrying guns, rather an odd metallic spear. The Man in Black charged at the nearest one and clothes-lined him to the ground. When the man tried to get up, a boot to the face put him down and out. The second attacker ran past the two grapplers and made a beeline for the place where Jane had entered the woods. A single shot rang out through the park. The man cried out briefly and dropped to the ground, his spear launching itself into the treeline. Johnny stood, gun still outstretched in his arm. He began to shake uncontrollably.

"We gotta go, brother," whispered the Man in Black. He took the gun from Johnny and pulled him toward the street. "Now!" He took off running with Johnny in tow. Johnny ran until his side ached and his breathing was reduced to desperate gasping. His heart was pounding in his ears. Finally after an eternity, the Man stopped and calmly hailed a taxi. He shoved Johnny into the cab's back seat and crawled in next to him. He gave the cabbie Johnny's address.

They rode in silence until arriving at Johnny's apartment. He'd tried to speak, but the Man had shook his head, silencing him. Still,

Johnny took a moment to check on his Charger before leading the way to his apartment. Flopping down on the couch, the Man finally introduced himself, "Tommy Page," he stated, offering Johnny a firm handshake.

"Johnny Evans," replied the scared young man.

"I know that, brother," laughed Page. "I've been watching you for a few days now."

"So can you please tell me what the Hell is going on?" said Johnny, angrily. "I'm not used to being attacked at the park, even if it seems totally natural to you."

"Calm down. I'll do my best to explain, but it's going to take a while. You got a beer?"

Chapter 8

"Dreams," began Page, "have never been fully understood. Some people think they are your brains way of exploring your fears and desires. Some think that dream are how your brain sorts out all the information that it receives while you're awake. Others think it's just a collection of random neurons firing while you rest. This is what I understand. There are alternate realities. When we dream, we have access to all of our memories from all of those realities, not just this one."

"Wait a minute. Define alternate reality," interrupted Johnny, "Like where we lost World War II and the Germans rule the world?"

"That could be one alternate reality. Picture a deck of cards that stretches forever in each direction. Your reality is the card right in the middle of the deck. The realities closest to you are very similar to your own. The Johnny Evans in those realities would be a virtual carbon copy of yourself. Maybe those versions of Johnny would have a small scar somewhere new. Maybe a few more miles on his car. Nothing major. As you move farther away the changes would grow. For example, ten realities away you'd still be mostly the same person. You'd still love that car of yours. You'd still have the same favorite TV shows and video games. But maybe you'd have a different couch or be in a different apartment in this building."

"How does this explain the strange dreams?" questioned Johnny.

"Maybe Johnny from fifteen realities away, Johnny +15, gets in a bar fight. You could dream that here since it's a memory from your total consciousness."

"So how do you know all of this?"

"There's a technique, called lucid dreaming, in which the dreamer knows that they are dreaming and can sometimes direct their dreams. Those who have mastered it become aware of the alternate realities that exist. It's still not perfect. I can't tell an alternate version of myself something, but when I dream, I remember much more and can often piece together events that took place in a different reality," continued Page. "When you get a small group of people together that all have this ability, you can get a very clear picture of things."

"So you work for the Dream Police?" laughed Johnny, despite the seriousness of the situation.

"I do not. But there are those that strive to control the direction of their own universe by making it match those around it. Another example: John Smith gets fired from his job as police chief. His replacement cracks a big case and a killer is put behind bars. In a nearby reality, John Smith doesn't get fired and the killer hasn't been caught. By nudging the universe and making sure Mr. Smith gets fired in every universe, the killer never gets away."

"But what if John Smith is destined to do something great as police chief a year from now?" questioned Johnny, "Who is to say what the future hold?"

"Exactly!" exclaimed Page, pounding a fist into his open palm, "That is exactly what I've been preaching for almost a year."

"To the Dream Police?"

"They call themselves the Guardians. It's a group of 20 members that have taken it upon themselves to steer humanity."

"And you are one of them?" asked Johnny quietly.

"I was. Until this situation demanded that I act."

"Jane," Johnny stated, "It's about Jane."

"The Guardians believe that she was meant to die. You travel plus or minus ten universes and she died as an infant in a terrible house fire. Suddenly last week, she started dying in the remaining universes as well. You've been dreaming each of those deaths. When she didn't die in this universe, the Guardians took notice."

"What harm can her living cause?" spat out Johnny, the anger growing inside him.

"The Guardians think that her living will change the course of your life in this universe."

"So what? What does it matter if one universe changes?"

"Johnny, you're not listening. I live in THIS universe. The Guardians that I know of live in THIS universe. They dream about how things are in those alternate realities and they want those events to happen here as well," explained Page, trying to find a way to make Johnny see the danger.

"So what's going on with me in those other realities? I haven't dreamed about anything unusual."

"I don't know what the Guardians think they've found either. I left the group when they started talking about eliminating Jane from her remaining universes," admitted Page. "It could be just about anything."

"And one man will make that big of a difference to justify murder?"

"The universes tend to normalize to each other. Did you ever have deja vu? Of course you have. Something happened in the majority of the realities around you, making it bound to happen here as well. When it does, you subconscious has already lived it in those other realities so you get that deja vu feeling. The Guardians have a better grasp of what has happened in the nearby universes and must have sensed something they didn't like."

Johnny's head was spinning with all the implications. Tommy Page saw this and decided it was time to turn in for the night. After Johnny turned in, Page carefully loaded his gun and placed it within reach before falling asleep on the couch.

Chapter 9

Johnny did not remember any of his dreams that night, although he desperately wished to do so. He awoke with a start and jumped out of bed. Peering through the doorway he was surprised to see that Tommy Page was not in his apartment. Johnny cautiously crept to the apartment door and looked through the peephole. A large freckle faced man with dark sunken eyes stared at him.

"Open the door, Johnny."

With a cry, Johnny scrambled backwards as the door burst open. He threw his arm in front of him in a vain attempt to stop the large military knife descending towards him. It struck his arm and embedded itself deep into the muscle. The pain was intolerable. Johnny screamed. The huge man pushed the knife further through his arm and used it to the pin the limb to the floor. Then he calmly drew a gun, pointed it at Johnny's head and pulled the trigger.

"Nooooooo!" screamed Johnny, sitting up in bed. He could still feel the pain in his arm, the fear of seeing the gun end his life. Sweating and shaking, he still took a minute to quickly dress before going out into his living room. Page was sleeping on the couch, but he quickly opened his eyes when he heard Johnny coming.

"What's wrong, brother?" he asked.

"I just dreamed about this huge guy with freckles killing me. He just came through the door, stabbed me then shot me," trembled Johnny, "It felt so real."

Page was already on his feet, gun in hand. "Was he about 6'0, 250lbs? Kind of a spiked haircut, blonde hair?"

"Yes!"

"Snake Samuels. The Guardian's hitman. Shit!"

"But it was just a dream," started Johnny, then realization hit him, "Damn. He killed me in another reality didn't he?"

"Probably. I told you, we're not entirely sure how dreams work, but from what I understand that is likely what happened," confirmed Page.

"Well, then why didn't he kill me here?" questioned Johnny.

"Because I was here and he knows it. Exactly in how many universes do the tow of us know each other? I don't have the answer for that."

"So I could dream about being killed over and over again. Swell," said Johnny, becoming angry. "We need to stop this."

After a quick breakfast, Johnny took a minute to check his email. There was a message from Adam Graves!

Mr. Evans,

I'm glad you enjoyed Hotel Hell. As you know, the book is based on a real life experience. I've always been interested in anything unusual, and your dreams certainly qualify. If you are available, I'm doing a book signing on Saturday at the City Center Mall in Johnsville, not too far from you. Hope you can make it.

Adam

"This is the answer!" Johnny shouted, showing the email to Page. "We need to go see this guy. Today. It's only an hour away."

"Johnny, this is an author looking to pimp out some more book sales. Not someone who can help us."

"Have you read *Hotel Hell*? If even a small part of it is fact, it represents proof in ghosts. That's almost easier to swallow than the Dream Police."

"Good point. It's your call. We don't know where to find Jane anyways," replied Page, giving in.

"She always seems to find me. Let's hope she does again, today."

Johnny was in his element, driving his black Charger down the highway weaving in and out of cars effortlessly. He smiled as he glanced at Page in the passenger seat. His curly hair was blown straight back from the wind coming through the open window and a look of terror was plastered on his face. A semi rode next to a camper in front of them, blocking both lanes. Page relaxed his grip on the side of the door sensing an inevitable slowdown coming.

Caressing the steering wheel for a brief moment, Johnny pressed down firmly on the accelerator. The engine roared and the car jumped forward. It closed rapidly on the rear of the semi. Page paled. At last moment, Johnny pulled the wheel to the left and passed on the semi on the side of the road, gravel spitting off his wide rear tires. A bump on the shoulder caused Johnny's butt to momentarily become airborne, but he laughed as they swerved back onto the road in front of the truck.

"What's wrong with you?" screamed Page, "Do you want to die?"

"No chance of that here. This car and me are one and the same. I know exactly what she can do. Not real happy that she probably got a few scratches from the gravel, but if my life is going to end, I might as well enjoy driving her while I can."

Adam Graves was not what Johnny expected. His book had portrayed him as a brave adventurer crossing swords with an evil ghost. In reality he looked more like the drummer for a garage band. His dark rimmed glasses contrasted his spiked blue hair. His frame leaned toward the pudgy side and his clothes seemed many sizes too big, obscuring any real shape to his body. His eyes were bright and his smile was easy as he interacted with his fans.

Page had chosen to wander the book store rather than wait in line to meet Mr. Graves. Johnny watched with amusement as children and adults alike gave Page a wide berth. He was still dressed in mostly black leather. With a three day beard and his hair even wilder than normal from the car ride, Tommy Page looked every bit the role of crazy biker or pro wrestler.

"Hey you!" came a female voice from behind Johnny. His heart skipped a beat as he turned, looking for Jane. Instead, Joanna Anderson stood smiling at him. She was dressed in a conservative top and faded jeans, with painted toes peeking out from her sandals. He tried to smile, but faltered. She noticed the disappointment on his face and her smile faded. Johnny quickly recovered.

"Hey! I didn't know you were an Adam Graves fan," he said.

"Yeah. There's a lot you don't know about me. Too bad you didn't stick around to find out the other night."

"Ouch. I guess I deserve that," replied Johnny quietly.

"Yeah, you do," she sighed. "I hope you worked everything out with your ex."

"It's still complicated," he admitted. "But I did have a good time with you," he said, offering his hand, "Forgive me?"

She hesitated only a moment before shaking his hand. "Deal. Let's start over." There were still about a dozen people in line ahead of them. "Are you getting him to sign your copy of *Hotel Hell*?" she asked.

"Uh, yeah. And I've got some questions for him. We've been talking via email and he invited me down."

"You KNOW Adam Graves? Cool!" she squealed, locking her arm around his, pressing herself close to him, "You have GOT to introduce me."

"Well, I don't exactly know him. But he is interested in some of the dreams I've been having lately."

"About your ex?"

"Kind of. It's a long story."

Joanna looked around uncomfortably and was relieved that their turn with Adam Graves had arrived. Stepping in front of Johnny, she proudly presented her book for him to sign. Adam looked her up and down, nodding his head in silent approval. With a smile, he thanked her. Johnny stepped to the table and set down his copy of *Hotel Hell*. He offered a hand to Adam, who accepted.

"Johnny Evans. Nice to meet you, Mr. Graves. I'd emailed you about some strange dreams..." said Johnny.

"Hey, Yeah! Nice to meet you too. And it's just Adam, please. How's it going?"

"Well," started Johnny, looking around for Page, "It's gotten stranger. Any chance you want to talk about it somewhere else?"

"I'll be done here in about an hour. Meet me at the bar a few stores down?"

"Sounds good," answered Johnny, then noticing Joanna staring at him, "Hey, is okay for my friend Joanna to come too?"

Adam smiled, "The more the merrier."

Chapter 10

An hour later the four of them sat in a booth, each with a beer bottle in front of them. Page sat on the outside with Johnny next to him, Joanna on the inside and Adam next to her. Johnny felt a pang of jealousy every time that Joanna touched Adam's forearm as they talked. After a few minutes of small talk, Johnny got into his story. Joanna looked perturbed and disbelieving, but Adam grew more excited as Johnny and then Page went into details about the Guardians and the alternate universes. When Johnny finally finished, he sat back and let out a deep breath.

"Incredible," started Adam. "That is incredible. So when was the last time you saw Jane?"

With a glance at Joanna, Johnny spoke, "After the party, in the park."

"And have you dreamed of her since?"

"Nope."

"Interesting. Mr. Page, what do you think will happen if Jane just drives to a different state and starts her life over?"

"Well, the Guardians believe," began Page.

"No," interrupted Adam, "What do YOU think will happen?"

"I think she's probably doomed to die. Unless, of course, she isn't going to accomplish anything of significance in her life, then maybe she'll live."

"Because if she does something monumental it would make this universe too different from the ones near it?" asked Adam, searching for clarity. An idea was beginning to form in his mind.

"Exactly."

"What if the opposite happens? What if this reality bleeds over into the others?"

"It doesn't work that way," said Page.

"I don't think so either, but we can't be sure. Want to hear my theory?" asked Adam.

"Yes!" said Johnny.

"I think that if the reality changes too much, the distance become greater between it and the ones around it. I think most people would get cut off from their consciousness from those other universes. If the realities stretch each direction into infinity, at some point they would become so different from our own, that we'd be having crazy dreams all the time as we remembered them."

"Possibly," said Page slowly.

"So if we can keep Jane alive and if that changes our world, then eventually, the Guardians and everyone else would quit dreaming of the worlds without Jane."

Page shook his head to clear his thoughts. "I don't know. The Guardians never told me why they think Jane is so critical. Maybe it's just because she only survived in a handful of universes."

Adam shrugged and finished his beer. Waving to the waitress, he ordered another round for the table. "In any event, my suggestion is that you find out."

"How do I do that?" asked Johnny.

"Lucid Dreaming," answered Adam. "Where you try to keep your consciousness alert while you dream. It's a technique that is becoming more common and with practice you can control what you are dreaming. If dreams are really memories from other universes, you might be able to pick and choose which ones you experience, therefore answering the question of why you and Jane are of special interest to the Guardians. I'll send you some links with instructions on how to start."

"Thank you," said Johnny, "Thank you so much. I hope that it works."

Page grumbled thanks, still not believing that this was the right path to pursue. While they finished their drinks, Adam flirted more with Joanna. As they talked about his books, she was more than a little starstruck. When it came time to go, Adam asked her if she wanted to talk more in his hotel room. With her cheeks flushing, she accepted.

Turning to Johnny, she said, "Don't tell my dad."

"Who's your dad?" asked Johnny, confused.

"Felix. Your boss," she laughed, "I thought you knew that. I figured it's why you didn't chase me harder."

"That tool bag is your father?" slipped out before Johnny could stop himself. "Sorry. But the man is hard to work for."

"Harder to live with. In any case, no need to tell dear old dad that his sweet daughter left the bar with an older man," she smiled.

"Understood."

They shook hands again with Adam and watched as he put his arm around Joanna and led her away. Page stopped at the bar and ordered himself a shot before they left.

"To keep me calm on the ride home."

Adam followed through on his promise. When Johnny arrived home and checked his email, there was a message from Adam that included links to several sites on Lucid Dreaming. He also thanked Johnny for introducing him to Joanna. Johnny sifted through the sites, desperate. Most sites talked about calm breathing, physical cues to remind your brain to keep its consciousness active and what to do if you began to wake up before you wanted to. It was fascinating stuff.

Page tried to keep an open mind, but was more concerned that they didn't know where Jane was. He was inclined to go search for her, but instead chose to park himself on Johnny's couch for another night.

Johnny prepared for bed earlier than normal. One of the techniques to have a lucid dream was to make sure your mind wasn't so exhausted that you lost control. He lay back in his bed and closed his eyes. Concentrating on deep, steady breathing he tapped his thumb and forefinger together every fifth breath. Counting slowly backwards from one hundred, Johnny fell asleep.

Chapter 11

Johnny was at the park again. It was still dark outside. Moving away from the swings where Page had shot one of the attackers, Johnny felt nervous. He took a deep breath and suddenly knew where he was. He began to pick up speed as he moved into the woods behind the park. Tree branches tore at his arms as we recklessly sped through. Emerging into a backyard, he looked up and saw it. The Treehouse. He'd been here before. With Jane.

Trembling, he climbed the boards nailed to the tree that formed a makeshift ladder. At the top, he pulled himself inside. Jane smiled at him from the corner. She was wearing jean shorts, a grey sweatshirt. Her hair was tangled and her face had small scratches, likely from the same trees that had cut into his arms. Silently, he sat down next to her and cupped her face with his hands. They kissed.

"Oh, Johnny," she cried, "I was wondering when you'd come."

"I'm here, Jane. I'm here."

The lovers embraced again. Jane snuggled her head into his chest and he wrapped his arms around her tightly. He wondered to himself why he would ever leave her. As he tightened his grip on her, he interlaced his fingers. As his thumb met his forefinger, clarity struck him.

"We're dreaming!" he said.

"What?" she replied, confused.

"Dreaming. We're asleep," he said, getting excited, "And I know it!"

"What do you mean, we're dreaming and you know it?"

Johnny didn't answer. Instead he was repeating something under his breath, over and over. Jane strained to here it. "Bright sunny day, bright sunny day, bright sunny day," he repeated again and again.

The world lit up outside. Sunlight streamed into the treehouse. Birds chirped. The temperature warmed.

"How did you do that?" she said, scared, but not moving from his side.

"We're asleep. This isn't real. It started as a memory, but I've gained control. I've been studying Lucid Dreaming."

"How is it possible that we are dreaming together?"

"I think that when we dream, our subconscious, maybe our souls, are all in the same place. We have the memories of all our realities here." He started to explain what he had learned between Tommy Page and Adam Graves, but the the world started to go dark. Straining to open his eyes in the dream world, but not in the real world, Johnny realized he was losing control.

"Jane, I'm going to wake up. I'm not sure if I can get back here again. I'll come to you tomorrow. Stay put and stay safe," he said, struggling to get out each word without waking up.

"I love you, Johnny."

Johnny woke up and looked at the clock. It was only 1:00am. Immediately, he settled back onto his bed and tried to get back to sleep. His mind continued to race at the implications of Lucid Dreaming. He couldn't force himself to relax enough to fall back asleep. When he finally did drift off, he dreamed of work. He dreamed of never ending piles of paperwork and desperately trying to finish it to get out, but never quite getting there.

At 7:00am he awoke.

Carefully he shook Page's shoulder, fearful that the large man would go for his gun before realizing that it was only Johnny. Page did wake with a start, but his hand did not go for his weapon. Explaining that he had dreamed where to find Jane, they quickly dressed, Page in his jeans and black vest, Johnny in his work clothes.

They sped toward the park. This time Page wasn't concerned with Johnny's driving. He was loading his gun and preparing for a fight. However, when they stopped the car near the park, all was quiet. In fact, it was a perfect morning. The air was cool, but the sun was shining bright. Birds chirped and a light breeze brought the scent of flowers to them. Page raised an eyebrow at Johnny, but diligently followed him into the woods.

Taking the same path he had in his dream, Johnny marched forward. Unlike his dream, he took his time and avoided the cutting branches that had sliced into him. Minutes later, they stood before the treehouse. It was almost exactly like the dream. Johnny did notice a few differences. The rungs of the ladder were painted different colors and a small blanket hung over the doorway. Motioning for Page to stand guard, Johnny began a slow, cautious climb to the top. He hesitated before pulling aside the blanket. Peering inside, he smiled as he saw Jane sleeping peacefully in the corner.

He crept forward and gently kissed her on the cheek. Her eyes fluttered open, and then widened in recognition.

"Oh, Johnny!" she cried, sitting up and throwing her arms around him. "Did you dream about us too? Was it real?"

"We were together in the dream. It was real."

They held each other silently until Page's whispered shout from below broke their embrace.

"Johnny? Is everyone okay?"

Johnny stuck his head out and looked down at Page with a goofy smile on his face. "She's here. She's fine. We'll be right down."

Moments later the three of them were making their way back through the woods toward where the car was parked. Johnny gave a proper explanation this time about everything he had learned. Jane listened intently, never once arguing. After everything that had happened, she was willing to accept any explanation.

As they pulled away from the park, from the backseat, Jane said quietly, "So, I'm supposed to be dead?"

"No," said Page, still riding shotgun, "Just because you died in other realities, it doesn't doom you in this one."

"But these Guardian guys think it should?"

"That's the gist of it."

"They won't hurt you," said Johnny, "I won't let them."

Johnny parked his car in the corner of the Walker Industries parking ramp, in his usual spot. Page had vetoed the idea of taking Jane back to Johnny's apartment. Since Snake Samuels had found the apartment in an alternate universe, there was a great chance that he would find it here too. Johnny led Page and Jane to a small storeroom in the plant itself. He felt foolish pointing out the J-38 robotic arms that he had programmed, but Jane seemed impressed. Giving Jane a passionate kiss goodbye, Johnny left them alone and took the elevator upstairs to the 3rd floor office.

Walking it, he spotted Colton talking to Felix. Johnny moved quickly to get to his desk before Felix could notice him. Dean and Jose were waiting for him.

"So did you bang the bosses daughter?" smirked Jose.

"No, man. He ditched her at my house. Went running off into the night," said Dean. "What was your problem, bro?"

"I had things to do. And I saw Joanna again just yesterday," answered Johnny truthfully.

"And just where did you see her, Evans?" injected Felix from behind him, "Because she didn't come home last night!"

"Sorry, sir. I ran into her in Johnsville, at a book store. We had a drink afterward, but I left before she did."

"Evans, if I find out that you did anything inappropriate with my daughter..." he trailed off, unable to think of a work friendly way to finish the sentence. "And you," he said pointing to Dean, "Will never send her another text message again. Work starts in two minutes. You all better be at your desks, ready to work, when it does." Felix stomped off, his face red with suppressed rage.

"What did you do?" whispered Johnny.

"After you took off and left her there, we had a few more drinks and one thing led to another. I guess Felix must have seen the text where I let her know that I found her underwear," Dean laughed. He left for his cubicle.

Jose stuck around, "So where did you go after the party?"

"I don't have time to explain it all," Johnny said, glancing at the clock in the corner of his computer, "But Jane, the dream girl, is in storage room B with the Man in Black."

Eyes wide, Jose whispered, "No shit? Really?"

"Get to work people! You're on my time now!" boomed Felix.

Keeping a careful eye on Felix, Johnny and Jose chatted via Private Messages. Jose's skepticism quickly turned to curiosity and then to apprehension as Johnny filled him in on the details of the last few days.

Jose: So what are you going to do now?
Johnny: Not sure. Maybe burn some PTO and get out of town

Jose: What about this Snake guy? Sounds like a scary hombre
Johnny: That's why I want to leave town
Jose: Felix!

Johnny quickly minimized the chat window and set to work on the newest instructions for the J-38. Felix walked behind him and peered at the computer screen from over his shoulder.

"Good work, Evans," said Felix, "But what is this nonsense at the end? Isn't that wasting time?"

"But Mr. Anderson, don't forget to count how many time the hydraulic tubing gets wrapped around the shaft of the arm. I added the commands to rotate the actuator back before restarting the sequence," said Johnny.

Felix nodded and stood upright and shouted to the entire office, "At the end of every sequence, let's reset the arm exactly how it started. That way no wires or tubing will ever get wrapped up."

"Great idea, boss!" said Colton from the corner.

"Thanks!" answered Felix, "Just doing my job." He moved on to the other end of the office.

Jose: That douche stole your idea
Johnny: I'm used to it. Who cares?
Jose: You should.
Johnny: I've got more important things to worry about. Let him have it. I don't want his job anyway, so he might as well take the credit.

Chapter 12

The warning siren jerked them all back to reality.

"Is that the fire alarm?" yelled out a woman.

"No, it's the terrorism alert!"

The security guard ran past the office doorway, "Gunfire down by the robots! Get under your desks and stay put!"

Felix, as a volunteer emergency responder, instantly ran after the guard to give any help he could. Johnny hesitated only for a second before deciding he had to make sure that Jane was not in danger.

"Where the hell are you going?" questioned Dean.

"To check on Jane," answered Johnny.

"Don't be stupid. She's not worth it," said Dean, crouching under his desk.

Johnny had no time to argue. With a sad look, he left the office and ran down the hallway toward the stairs. He heard footsteps following him. Turning to thank Dean for coming, he instead saw Jose sprinting toward him.

"Thanks, buddy."

"Come on, hombre, we got to save your woman," panted Jose.

The two men raced down the stairs two at a time, using the handrails to swing around the corners. Throwing open the battered grey door at the first level, the sound of gunfire filled the air. They huddled down in the doorway. Johnny could see Tommy Page across the room with Jane hiding behind him. They were squatting behind a file cabinet. Page had his gun drawn and was taking random shots across the room.

From behind one of the robot arms, a huge blonde man was taking careful aim toward the file cabinet. It was the man from his dreams, Snake Samuels. He was dressed in a faded green army uniform. Two other men, dressed similarly, were crouched near him. The dark haired one began to slowly move toward the wall, while the other man, wearing an army helmet, began a crawl toward Page and Jane.

Jane screamed in terror.

"Jane!" cried out Johnny.

Snake turned his gun toward the sound of Johnny's voice and fired. The bullet went high and ricocheted around the stairwell. Johnny and Jose sprinted behind one of the large industrial machines and hid.

"Johnny, get the hell out of here!" shouted Page. "Now!"

Two guards and Felix burst through the far door.

"Hands up!" shouted one of the guards.

Snake Samuels shot at him, causing the guard to dive back through the open door. The remaining guard hit the ground, as did Felix. The dark haired invader dropped his pistol and swung a machine gun from his back into a firing position. He sprayed the area where Page and Jane were hiding with bullets.

"No!" screamed Johnny.

Felix launched himself toward the machine gunner. Snake ran toward Felix. Page, bleeding, poked out and fired toward Snake. Everything was a confusing cluster of smoke, gunfire and screaming.

Jose snaked his hand around the machine and pressed the large green button. The robotic arms came to life. Though there was no product on the assembly line, the arms began their programmed routine as the empty conveyer began to move.

Page's shot caught Snake in the shoulder, spinning him to the ground. The machine gunner caught Felix in the air and twirled, launching Felix toward the conveyer belt. The man with the army helmet fired his gun and Page's chest exploded in a bloody mess. Jane screamed and ran toward Johnny.

One of the guards fired and the machine gunner fell to the floor. Page struggled to his knees and got off a final round before collapsing face first. His shot caught the man in the helmet in the throat. He died in a horrible gurgling noise.

Jane reached Johnny and Jose. They stood to run for the door. Snake Samuels stood, his gun calmly aimed at Jane, despite the blood running from his shoulder. He smiled and started to pull the trigger. A scream from behind him caused him to turn.

Felix was on the conveyer belt and being torn apart by the robotic arms. One arm had grasped his right leg and twisted it almost 360 degrees. The conveyer moved him to the next set of robots. One arm plucked him into the air by his left shoulder, the force crushing his muscle and bone into pulp. The second arm drove a long, seven inch screw into his chest. The first arm set him back onto the conveyer. The last thing that Felix would see was a large metal stamp that read "Walker Industries" as it was coming down onto his forehead.

Using the distraction, Johnny, Jane and Jose made it the doorway, slamming the huge steel door being them.

Jose smashed the glass of the emergency fire equipment. Looping the long flat hose around the door handle and the rail of the stairs, he managed to tie the door shut. Snake was screaming on the other side of the door.

"She has to die! I will find her!" He fired random shots through the narrow opening.

Jose called 911 from his cellphone as Johnny and Jane sped off in the black Charger. He remained hidden behind a shrub as Snake managed to escape and hopped into a steel grey pickup truck and raced out of the parking lot in the direction that Johnny had gone. He calmly gave the operator a description of the truck.

Chapter 13

"I don't think anyone will find us here," said Johnny. They were inside a run down motel room half way to Johnsville. They had checked in under Mr. and Mrs. Gordon and they had paid cash.

"I'm so sorry about your car, Johnny," said Jane before she stood up and went into the small bathroom.

Johnny knew that Snake Samuels was still out there and that Johnny's car was unique enough to give away their hiding place. They had abandoned the car in a seedy part of town and left the keys inside. Johnny hoped that whoever stole it led Samuels on a long goose chase.

He lay back on the dingy bed and examined the room. It was painted in a dark yellowish beige, reminiscent of the walls of his grandfather's retirement home. An ancient television sat atop a warped wooden stand. There was no other furniture in the room. Johnny dared not pull back the bedspread for fear of what lay underneath.

The toilet flushed and made a squealing noise followed by a clunking as the water in the sink ran briefly. Jane emerged from the bathroom, naked. Her face was flushed red and her nipples stood proudly as she crossed the room and climbed onto the bed with him. Straddling him, she bent and kissed him fiercely on the lips. Their tongues intertwined passionately.

"Jane," he started.

"Shhh," she quieted him, kissing him again, "Just go with it." She slowly undid his belt as his hands slid over her entire body.

When they had finished making love, she had put on his t-shirt and cuddled up to next to him. They fell asleep without talking.

Johnny ran from room to room looking for Jane. Where was she? Every room seemed identical. White and sterile.

"Jane!" he screamed. There was no answer. "Jane!" he yelled again.

"I'm here!" came a quiet voice, seemingly miles away, yet it was something. Johnny ran in that direction. He came to a wide open floor of the building. Large windows lined one entire wall. Through them he could see the city spread out before him. He was in an office building, evidently yet to be filled.

Jane was standing along the wall of windows. Snake Samuels had one arm wrapped around her throat, the other held a large hunting knife poised to cut her open.

"No!" yelled Johnny.

"Stop right there, boy," snarled Snake, "Or I'll cut her throat right now and this can all be over."

"What do you want from us?" cried Johnny.

"I need to know. Is she with child?"

"What are you talking about?"

"Is she pregnant?" screamed Snake as tears streamed down Jane's face, "Did you have sex with her?"

Confused, Johnny answered truthfully, "Yes, we did. In the motel room."

"Damn!" cursed Snake, "That makes it more complicated. Now you both have to die."

"Why? Why do we have to die?" pleaded Johnny.

"Because she isn't supposed to be here. In this universe, Jane Jordan died at the age of two in a house fire."

"No," Jane stammered, "I didn't. I ran out the back door and hid in the woods. A few days later a Cub Scout troop found me and I went to live with my Aunt Rachel."

"No," stated Snake firmly, "You died. They found your body. Then somehow you jumped from another reality to this one, confusing the hell out of the police. There's a grave in the cemetery for an unknown child. It's your grave."

"I thought Page said that in the universes close to this one, Jane was alive, at least until recently?" questioned Johnny, suddenly aware that he was dreaming. Somehow, he, Jane and Snake were sharing a dream.

"That is true," grumbled Snake, "In those realities, she escaped the fire and was sent to live with her Aunt. Except in reality +7. In that reality, Jane Jordan vanished when she was two. Presumed dead. No body ever found. She jumped from that reality to this one."

"How is that possible?" cried Jane.

"We do not know. But it makes you very dangerous. And now that Mr. Evans here has connected with you in a physical way, we are concerned that another version of you will try to jump to this reality again to be with him. The Guardian's computer has predicted that you would become pregnant and that your offspring with Mr. Evans would be considered dangerous."

"Why would my offspring be dangerous?" asked Johnny, desperately trying to stall as he formulated a plan of escape.

"Because you are dangerous. You have begun to grasp the rules of the universe. Combined with her ability to jump realities, you could disrupt the natural course of all reality."

"Maybe the natural course of reality is that humans learn to control it," spat Johnny. "You have no right to stop that!"

"We are the Guardians. That is why we exist. To preserve the natural order."

"How did you get into our dreams? Page said that dreams were us remembering what we did in nearby realities. How are you interacting with us now?"

"Mr. Page was incorrect. The dream world, this world, knows no bounds. It is not restrained by time, nor is it restrained to only a single reality. It is something like Heaven. It is where your soul lives. You are not dreaming right now, in the traditional sense. Your consciousness, your soul, is in between realities right now, as if you had died."

"If this is Heaven," started Johnny, "Where are our family and friends? Where is God?"

"I said it is something like Heaven. What I do know is that if you die here, your soul disappears for good. Where it goes, I do not know, nor do I care," finished Snake.

Johnny continued to rub his fingers together as he had studied for Lucid Dreaming. He concentrated on creating a distraction. He closed his eyes and tried to imagine a loud explosion. Nothing happened. He opened his eyes. He was back in the hotel, with Jane asleep aside beside him.

Crying out in a panic, Johnny squeezed his eyes shut and tried to force himself back to sleep. Jane whimpered next to him. His mind was racing. Johnny couldn't get back to sleep. He tried to wake Jane, first shaking her gently, then in desperation he violently shook her. Nothing would wake her.

Johnny looked around the room. He could see nothing that would get him back to sleep in this excited state. Jane cried out again in her sleep. Johnny took a deep breath, put his head down, and ran toward the wall. The crown of his head struck the wall and he fell back. His vision swam and darkness began to close in. Pain shuddered through his body, yet he maintained consciousness. He staggered to his feet and gave it another go. Abandoning any restraint, he rammed into the wall with a sickening thud. He passed out.

Jane's scream woke him. Johnny opened his eyes to find himself back in the office building of the Dream World. Jane knelt about ten feet away from him. Snake stood over her, a large knife held ready to strike.

"No!" bellowed Johnny, "You will not harm her!" Johnny launched himself, pushing Jane out of the way as Snake plunged the knife downward. The blade caught Johnny behind the shoulder and cut him all the way down to his hip before the knife was torn from Snake's hand.

The pain was incredible. His head spun, but he managed to grasp Snake by the neck and yank him to the ground.

The two men wrestled. Johnny managed to roll on top of Snake, but before he could gain control, Snake sank his fingers into Johnny's wound. The pain caused Johnny to release his grip and Snake threw him backwards. The large man scrambled on top of Johnny and locked his hands around his throat. Johnny's sight began to fade. Darkness closed in from the corners of his vision. All he could see was the face of Snake Samuels, red with anger.

Snake suddenly released his throat, a curious look on his face. He froze and then toppled over. Jane stood behind him, holding the bloody knife. Her eyes locked onto Johnny through the tears. He slowly stood up and embraced her.

"What are we going to do?" she asked, "There are more Guardian's. It's only a matter of time before they find us. We can't protect ourselves in the real world or the Dream World. Not forever."

"I wish there was a world where the Guardian's didn't exist," replied Johnny. "Surely in one of the millions of alternate realities out there, we're living in peace together."

An idea crossed his mind. He concentrated on that idea. A world where they would be safe. The wall of windows suddenly sprang to life. Each pane showed an identical picture of his life.

"Johnny," said Jane, "What are you looking at?"

"The windows! Don't you see? They are showing us other realities. We can find a safe place."

"I don't see anything Johnny. All I see is blackness."

Johnny began to walk along the windows. The office seemed to grow as he moved. The row of windows had the slightest curve to it. The rest of the room faded away. With Jane beside him, he began to run. Suddenly the row of windows turned dark.

"It's beautiful!" she cried out, pointing to one of the dark panes. Turning to Johnny, she saw him sadly shake his head. He saw nothing here.

They walked for miles attempting to find a world that they could both live in. Finally weariness set in and they stopped.

"The worlds I see as dark, I can just feel that I am not alive there," said Johnny.

"I understand. When I look into a dark window, all I feel is dread," answered Jane.

Johnny stood in front of a window pane that glowed golden for him. He tried to see further into the world. He reached his hand through the glass. He felt warmth and happiness. He moved his face closer, trying to see more. He pushed his arms outward and the window magically stretched wider. We could easily step through now. He turned and saw Jane with a tear running down her cheek. This world was not for her. In anger, he pushed against the window frame and cursed.

The entire row of windows spun, as if he had swiped the screen of a smartphone. Over and over again his spun the windows. Millions passed them, alternating light and dark. He stopped.

Jane reached her hand into one of the brightly lit worlds.

"Does it feel cold when you reach into the dark worlds?" asked Johnny.

"I don't know. I'm afraid to try."

Realization dawned on him. "Are you saying that this world is lit for you?"

"Yes!" she cried, "You too?"

"Yes, the next twenty or so windows are lit for me."

"Same here."

They slowly walked along the worlds that were open to them. They took turns reaching inside and describing the feelings that accompanied each. When they reached a consensus on which world gave them the best vibe, they joined hands and stepped through. Johnny felt the sensation of falling and then awoke.

Chapter 14

Johnny opened his eyes. Expecting to see the grimy hotel room, he was surprised to find himself laying in a king sized bed. The room was painted in blue and silver. Sunlight streamed in through the huge windows. Jane stirred next to him. She opened her eyes and sat up with a start.

She looked around and began to laugh. She leaned forward and kissed him. She began to climb out of the bed and then realized she was naked.

"I'm naked!" she giggled, but made no effort to hide herself from him.

"Not quite," he said quietly, pointing to her hand.

She held her hand up and saw an enormous wedding band. Her eyes went wide. A picture of the two of them, her in a gorgeous white gown and Johnny in a tuxedo sat in a gilded silver frame next to the bed.

"We're married," she said. "That's amazing. This must be our house."

They kissed again before she went into the bathroom. Johnny pulled open a dresser drawer and found some clothes. He was happy to discover that his body was fit and trim. He dressed quickly and was examining the room when Jane cried out from the bathroom. He rushed to her. She was now wearing a fluffy white robe and holding a small plastic stick in her hand.

"This was on the counter top," she said, offering it to him.

A large "+" was impossible to miss.

"Are we going to have a baby?" he said, incredulously.

"I think we are."

They looked at each other for a full minute before they both broke out in joyous laughter. He picked her up and carried her back to the bedroom.

Afterward, while she showered, Johnny picked up his cell phone and dialed the number that read "Work."

"Walker Enterprises," answered the voice on the phone. He cursed silently that he still worked at the same place. Dismissing it as the first negative of his new world, he spoke.

"This is Johnny Evans. I'm going to be a little late today. Can you please let the appropriate person know?"

"Yes sir, Mr. Evans. I don't think you have anything on your calendar today. I'll inform your secretary that you won't be in until later," said the woman on the phone.

"Um, thank you," said Johnny, slightly confused. *I have a secretary?* he thought.

Jane emerged from the bathroom looking fresh and clean. She dressed in a bright blue shirt and a flowered blouse. They exited the room to find the rest of their home just as grand as the bedroom. Parked in the driveway was Johnny's black Charger, looking as new as the day it rolled off the assembly line. He grinned as he held the door open for her. They drove off toward Johnsville.

"Are you sure this is the place?" asked Johnny.

"It's the only Thomas Page listed online. It must be," answered Jane.

They stood outside a strip mall. The stenciled lettering on the door read "Men's Yoga." A small bell clanged as they opened the door.

"Can I help you?" called a man from the back. Tommy Page stepped into the room wearing a black leotard.

"Page!" cried out Johnny.

"Do I know you?" said Page with a quizzical look on his face.

Jane quickly elbowed Johnny in the ribs. "We represent a group called the Guardians. We're interested in learning more about your yoga program," she said, carefully watching Page's face for any change. There was none.

"Awesome. Let me get you some literature and a DVD you can take with you. I've got programs for all levels of fitness," started Page, "And besides making you healthy, yoga will even help you sleep better."

They listened to his sales pitch for almost 30 minutes before leaving and assuring him that they would be in touch.

Jane rode with Johnny to Walker Enterprises. The very first parking spot, nearest the doors, read "Reserved for CEO John Evans." Johnny let out a long whistle.

"CEO, huh?" said Jane, "Looks like life is going pretty well."

Suddenly feeling under dressed, Johnny sheepishly entered the building. Employees called out to him.

"Hey, Mr. Evans!"

"Nice to see you, John."

"Hello, Mrs. Evans. Thanks again for dinner the other night."

He made his way to his old floor. He recognized most of the employees working there, including his friend Dean. Johnny scanned the cubicles for Jose, but did not find him.

"Mr. Evans, buddy, what can we do for you?" stammered Felix, nervously running his hands through his short gray hair.

"Felix! I never thought I'd be so happy to see you," laughed Johnny, "How's Joanna?" That drew a glare from Jane.

"She's good. Her and Adam are still working on their wedding plans. I hope you and Jane can make it."

"I'm sure we will be able to. Where's Jose?"

"Jose Fernandez? Is he supposed to be here today too?"

"I'm not sure. Have you seen him today?"

"I saw him heading upstairs to his office, as usual," replied Felix, confused.

Johnny glanced over Felix's shoulder and saw a memo signed, "J. Fernandez, Executive VP." Jose was his second in command.

"Never mind. It's all good. Hey, Felix, can you do me a favor? I want to set up a fitness program for the employees. Please ask Jose to call a place from Johnsville called "Men's Yoga." The owner, a Mr. Page, will be more than happy to work with us."

"No problem, Mr. Evans. I'll run upstairs and do that right away. Then I have to go down and audit the assembly line. Those robots scare me. I'm going to have nightmares tonight!"

Johnny laughed. Jane smiled.

The End

Made in the USA
Columbia, SC
01 November 2018